9/17

C1

WOULD YOU DARE
BE AN MMA
FIGHTER?

By Robert Kennedy

Gareth Stevens
PUBLISHING

Please visit our website, www.garethstevens.com. For a free color catalog of all our high-quality books, call toll free 1-800-542-2595 or fax 1-877-542-2596.

Library of Congress Cataloging-in-Publication Data

Names: Kennedy, Robert C., author.
Title: Would you dare be an MMA fighter? / Robert Kennedy.
Other titles: Would you dare be an Mixed Martial Arts fighter?
Description: New York : Gareth Stevens Publishing, [2017] | Series: Would you dare? | Includes index.
Identifiers: LCCN 2016028843| ISBN 9781482458145 (Paperback Book) | ISBN 9781482458152 (6 pack) | ISBN 9781482458169 (Library Bound Book)
Subjects: LCSH: Mixed martial arts--Juvenile literature. | Extreme sports--Juvenile literature.
Classification: LCC GV1102.7.M59 K46 2017 | DDC 796.8--dc37
LC record available at https://lccn.loc.gov/2016028843

First Edition

Published in 2017 by
Gareth Stevens Publishing
111 East 14th Street, Suite 349
New York, NY 10003

Designer: Laura Bowen
Editor: Therese Shea

Photo credits: Cover, p. 1 (fighters) Quinn Rooney/Getty Images Sport/Getty Images; cover, p. 1 (cage) Neil Lockhart/Shutterstock.com; cover, pp. 1–32 (background) Nik Merkulov/Shutterstock.com; cover, pp. 1–32 (paint splat) Milan M/Shutterstock.com; cover, pp. 1–32 (photo frame) Milos Djapovic/Shutterstock.com; pp. 5 (both), 13 (top), 30 Krabikus/Shutterstock.com; p. 7 Bealopez17/Wikimedia Commons; p. 8 Eugene Onischenko/Shutterstock.com; p. 9 Koji Aoki/Aflo/Getty Images; p. 11 Alex Trautwig/Getty Images Sport/Getty Images; pp. 13 (bottom), 17 sportpoint/Shutterstock.com; p. 15 Ivica Drusany/Shutterstock.com; p. 19 Jayne Kamin-Oncea/Getty Images Sport/Getty Images; p. 21 Diamond Images/Getty Images; p. 23 Real Deal Photo/Shutterstock.com; p. 24 Sakuoka/Shutterstock.com; p. 25 (gloves) Lumppini/Shutterstock.com; p. 25 (main) Oleg Romanko/Shutterstock.com; p. 27 (both) A.RICARDO/Shutterstock.com; p. 29 (main) agusyonok/Shutterstock.com; p. 29 (inset) NIKLAS HALLE'N/AFP/Getty Images.

Printed in China

CPSIA compliance information: Batch #CW17GS: For further information contact Gareth Stevens, New York, New York at 1-800-542-2595.

CONTENTS

DO YOU DARE?

Picture yourself in a ring surrounded by a cage. There's no way to escape. A crowd roars around you. Your **opponent** moves toward you. Your fight is about to begin. Would you dare to become a mixed martial arts (MMA) fighter?

DARING DATA

MMA bouts, or fights, are between only two people at a time. Both men and women practice MMA.

MIXING THE ARTS

A martial art is a fighting sport. Most martial arts began in East Asia. Mixed martial artists are skilled in many forms of martial arts, including karate, jujitsu, boxing, kickboxing, wrestling, judo, muay thai, and other **combat** sports.

DARING DATA

Judo is a fighting sport, but *judo* means "the gentle way" in Japanese!

Different martial arts focus on different skills. For example, karate uses striking, kicking, and blocking. Judo teaches grappling as well as how to fall so that you don't get hurt. Mixed martial artists use many parts of these sports in **competition.**

a karate kick

DARING DATA

"Grappling" means struggling with another person or holding them in a firm grip.

9

The idea for MMA came from a full-contact sport in Brazil called vale tudo. It uses many kinds of fighting styles, including wrestling and boxing. *Vale tudo* means "anything goes" in Portuguese. However, there are a few rules, such as not harming people's eyes.

DARING DATA

Vale tudo is a grappling sport.

11

IN THE CAGE

MMA competitions often take place in a cage. The cage isn't meant to keep fighters from running away. It protects them as well as the people watching. It would be easy for competitors to fall into the crowd and hurt themselves or others.

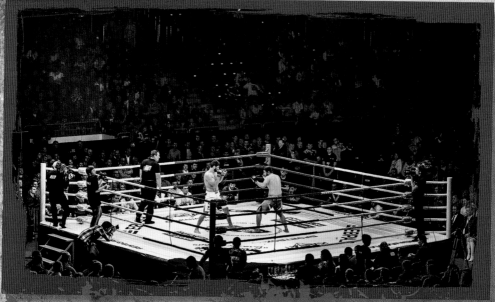

DARING DATA

Some MMA competitions take place in
a ring, similar to a boxing ring.

ROUND AND ROUND

Most MMA fights are made up of three rounds. Each round is 5 minutes long. That may not sound like a long time. However, it may only take a few seconds for one fighter to KO, or knock out, their opponent!

DARING DATA

Different MMA organizations may have more than three rounds.

15

ARE THERE RULES?

Some people think there are no rules in MMA. That's not true. The Unified Rules of Mixed Martial Arts guide many groups about how to keep competitions safe and fair. Not following certain rules may cost a fighter a point or even **disqualify** them.

DARING DATA

Sometimes fighters may break rules by accident.
Those who do so on purpose may be disqualified.

HOW TO WIN

Judges score MMA fights. The judges give points to fighters based on each fighter's **technique**. Different competitions score fights in different ways. One way is called the 10-Point Must System. The winning fighter's points must add up to 10.

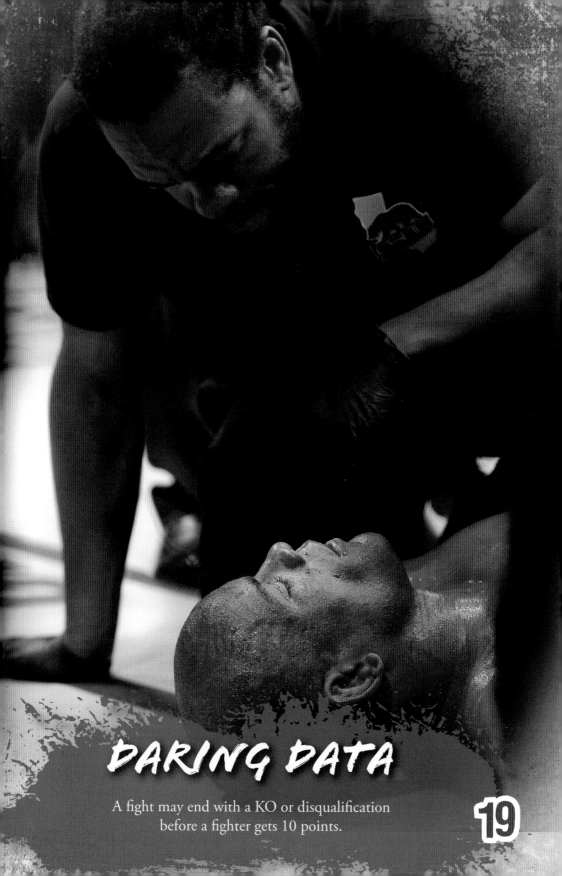

DARING DATA

A fight may end with a KO or disqualification
before a fighter gets 10 points.

19

WHAT'S A TKO?

"TKO" stands for "technical knock out." It's another way to end a fight. **Referees**, doctors, and the people in a fighter's corner can call a TKO. They may do this because a fighter isn't protecting himself and may get hurt.

DARING DATA

People in a fighter's corner may act as coaches between rounds or help them when they're hurt.

21

TIME TO
TRAIN

MMA fighters are highly skilled. Fighters have to train hard to learn not one but many martial arts. That's why there are special schools that teach MMA. Fighters also need to strengthen their bodies through certain workouts.

DARING DATA

Only people who have been trained in MMA should enter the ring. MMA is a dangerous sport without proper training.

There isn't much **equipment** needed for MMA, but the gear that is allowed can keep fighters safe. MMA fighters wrap their hands. They wear gloves over the wrap. They also wear mouth guards to protect their teeth.

DARING DATA

If a fighter loses a mouth guard, the referee may stop the fight or hand it back to the fighter during the fight.

ULTIMATE FIGHTING

"UFC" stands for "Ultimate Fighting Championship." It's a successful pro MMA organization. It holds more than 40 fights each year in many countries. Some of the best MMA fighters in the world take part in the UFC.

DARING DATA

The UFC is the fastest-growing sports organization in the world!

ARE YOU READY?

MMA fighters take on others in their weight class. Weight classes range from flyweight to superheavyweight. MMA competitions make each contest as fair as possible to show the fighters' skills. So, would you dare enter the MMA ring?

DARING DATA

As hard as opponents fight to win, they still shake hands or even hug at the end of a match.

DON'T DO IT!

Check out this list of what's not allowed in most MMA competitions:

- No knees to the head of a grounded opponent.
- No harming eyes.
- No biting.
- No fingers in an opponent's mouth.
- No hair pulling.
- No head butts.
- No striking or grabbing the throat.
- No grabbing the cage.
- No throwing an opponent outside of the cage.

FOR MORE INFORMATION

BOOKS

Johnson, Nathan. *Kickboxing and MMA*. Broomall, PA: Mason Crest, 2015.

Polydoros, Lori. *MMA Greats*. North Mankato, MN: Capstone Press, 2012.

Whiting, Jim. *Inside the Cage: The Greatest Fights of Mixed Martial Arts*. Mankato, MN: Capstone Press, 2010.

WEBSITES

Discover UFC
www.ufc.com/discover/sport
Learn about this MMA organization.

History of MMA
ockickboxing.com/blog/mma/history-of-mma-mixed-martial-arts/
Find out more about MMA's past.

GLOSSARY

combat: active fighting

competition: the act of trying to win something that someone else is also trying to win

disqualify: to make someone unable to get a prize or go further in competition because of a breaking of the rules

equipment: supplies or tools needed for a special purpose

opponent: a person competing against another in a contest

referee: a person who makes sure that players act according to the rules of a game or sport

technique: the way that a person performs movements or skills

INDEX